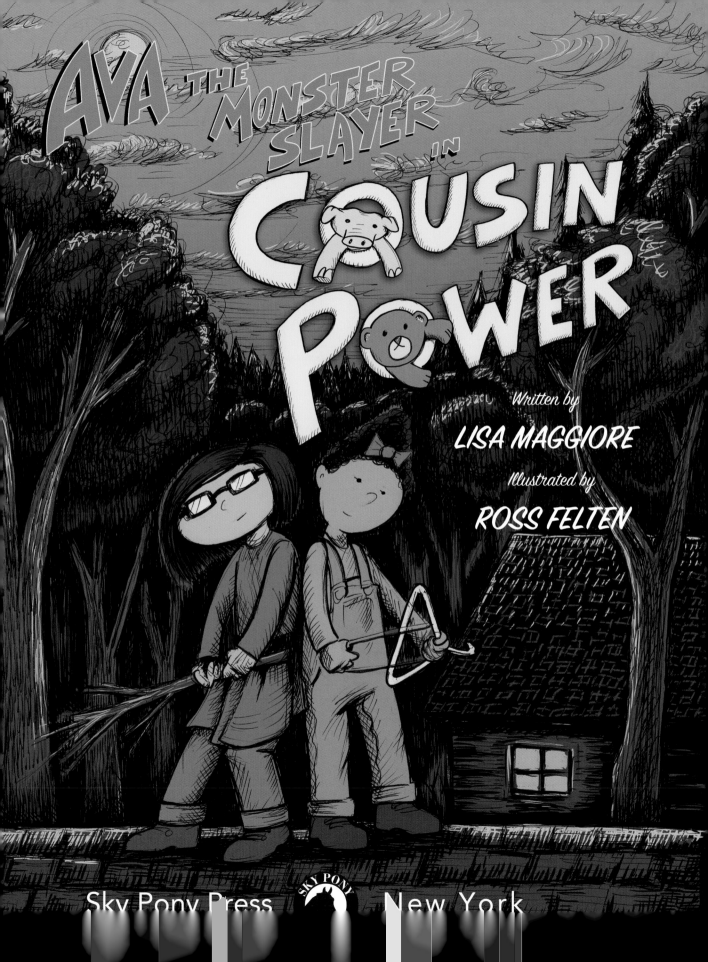

AVA THE MONSTER SLAYER in COUSIN POWER

Written by

LISA MAGGIORE

Illustrated by

ROSS FELTEN

Sky Pony Press   New York

Sky Pony Press books may be purchased in bulk at special discounts for sales promotion, corporate gifts, fund-raising, or educational purposes. Special editions can also be created to specifications. For details, contact the Special Sales Department, Sky Pony Press, 307 West 36th Street, 11th Floor, New York, NY 10018 or info@skyhorsepublishing.com.

Sky Pony® is a registered trademark of Skyhorse Publishing, Inc.®, a Delaware corporation.

Visit our website at www.skyponypress.com.

10 9 8 7 6 5 4 3 2 1

Manufactured in China, June 2019
This product conforms to CPSIA 2008

Library of Congress Cataloging-in-Publication Data is available on file.

Cover design and illustration by Ross Felton

Print ISBN: 978-1-5107-4810-1
Ebook ISBN: 978-1-5107-4811-8

Hi! I'm AVA, the FAMOUS Monster Slayer.

I rescued my favorite stuffed animal, Piggy, from the yucky basement monsters.

I love Piggy!

And my cousin, Sophia, loves her Teddy, too.

So, you can imagine how we felt this summer when Piggy and Teddy got lost in the woods!

Sophia and I went to an overnight camp for the first time. I was a little scared. Sophia was really scared.

But we had Piggy and Teddy to make us feel better.

On the first night, our cabin went on an evening hike.

We ate dinner on top of a grassy hill so we could watch the sunset.

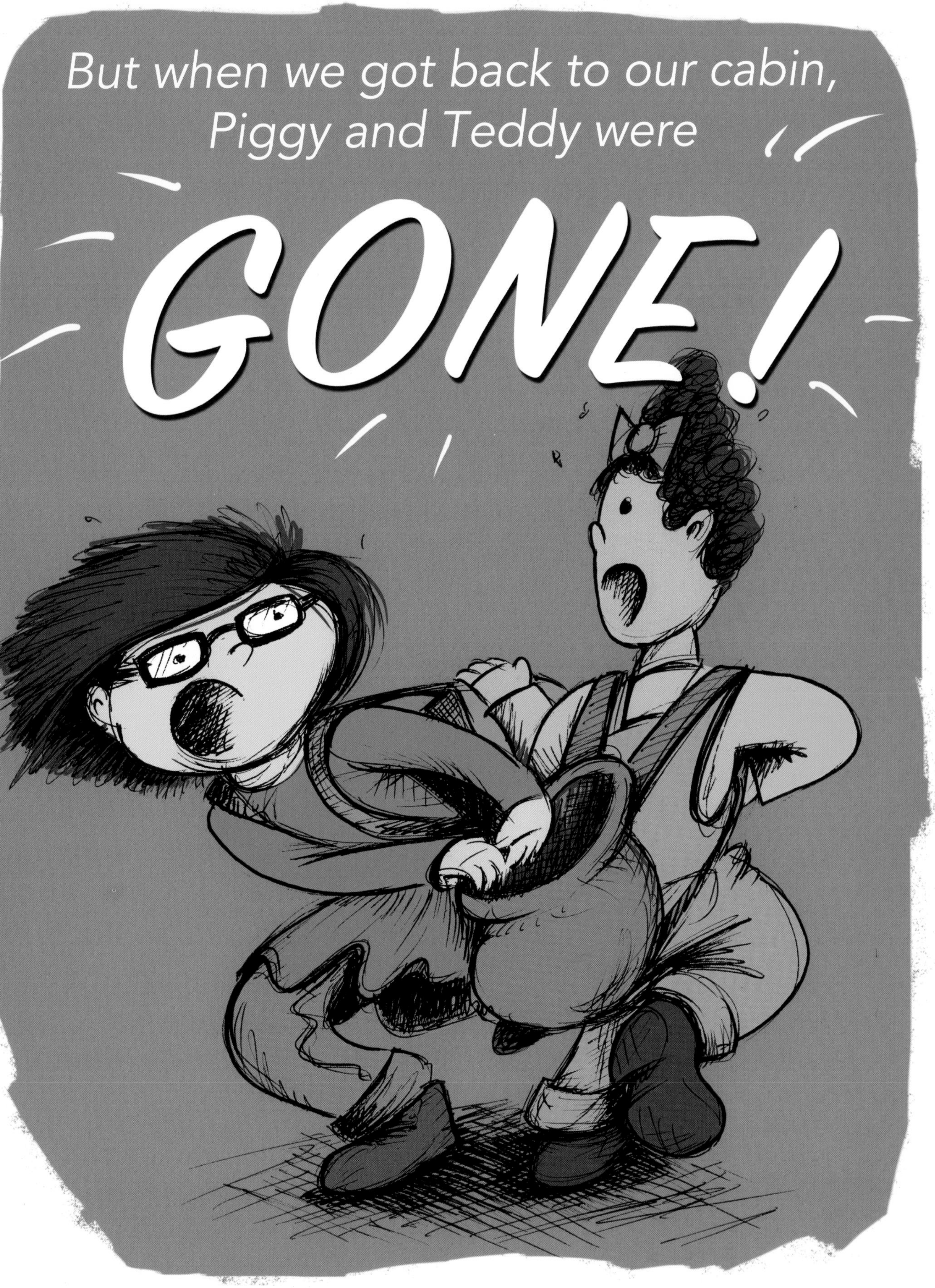
But when we got back to our cabin,
Piggy and Teddy were
GONE!

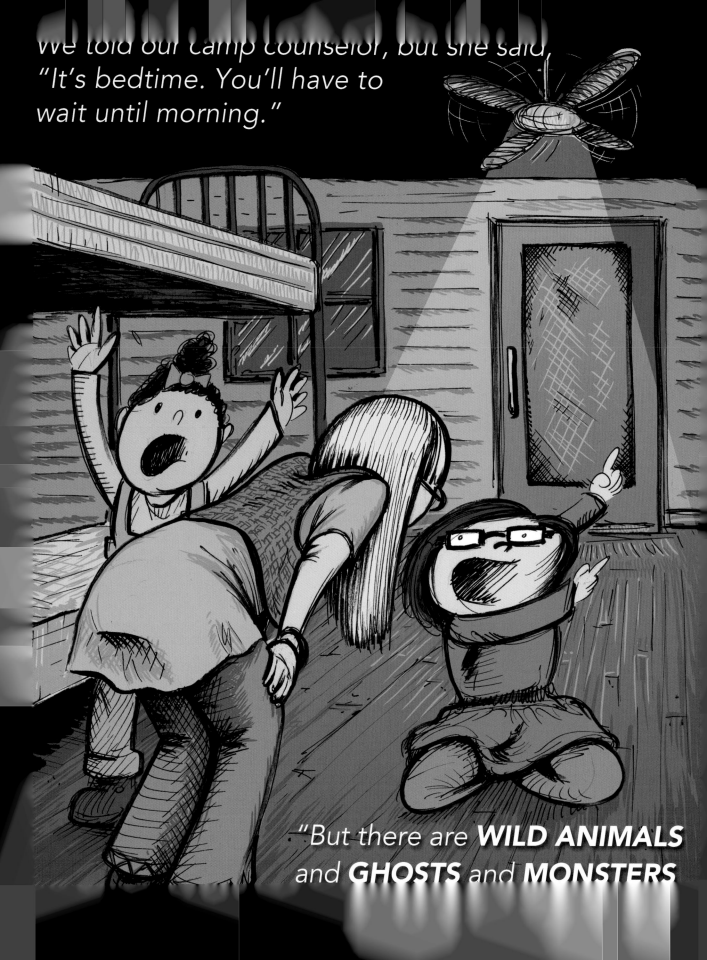

We stared into the woods. It was murky and gray. Piggy and Teddy must be so scared!

"What are you looking at?" asked the boys in the cabin next door.

"We lost our stuffed animals in there," said Sophia. "Can you help us find them?"

"Aren't you the FAMOUS Monster Slayer? Go get them yourselves."

I pushed my glasses up on my nose and took a deep breath.

I saved Piggy from the basement monsters, right? Even though I knew it was wrong, we had to sneak out to save them.

"BUT HOW?"

"We have to make weapons," I whispered.

I searched around and grabbed some sticks.

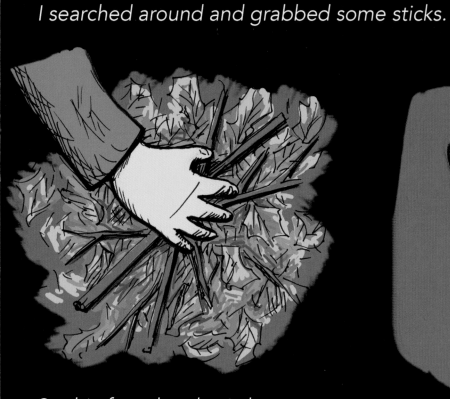

Sophia found a plastic hanger, a rubber band, and a bouncy ball.

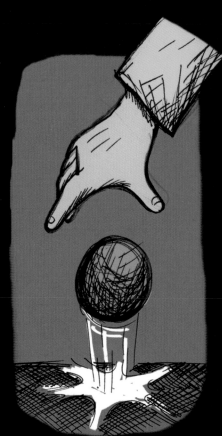

I HAVE AN IDEA!

Sophia took Pop Rocks from her candy stash and glue from the craft table.

She covered the bouncy ball with glue, then coated it with Pop Rocks.

I ran the RUBBER BAND along the HANGER to make a BOW

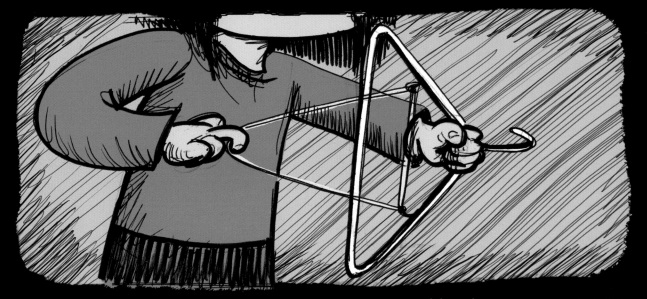

and broke some STICKS to make ARROWS.

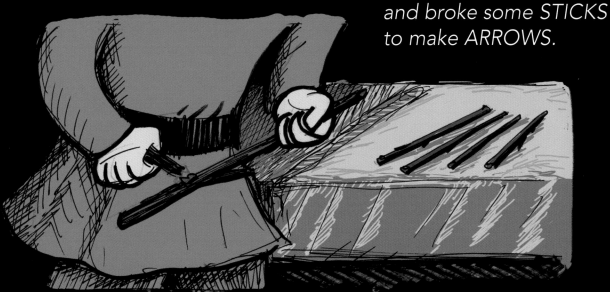

Sophia turned on her FLASHLIGHT but it **DIDN'T WORK.**

CLICK
CLICK

"We can't leave Piggy and Teddy. **THEY NEED US!** We must go into the deep, dark woods to save them!"

We crept outside and made our faces look

Sophia's hands were shaking.
I whispered, **"TAKE A DEEP BREATH,"** and showed her
how to aim the bow.

We tiptoed deeper.

"I smell nasty cheese," whispered Sophia.

"I smell dirty socks."

Something was in the tree above us. I took a deep breath.

We scared it so much that all its teeth fell out as it flew away.

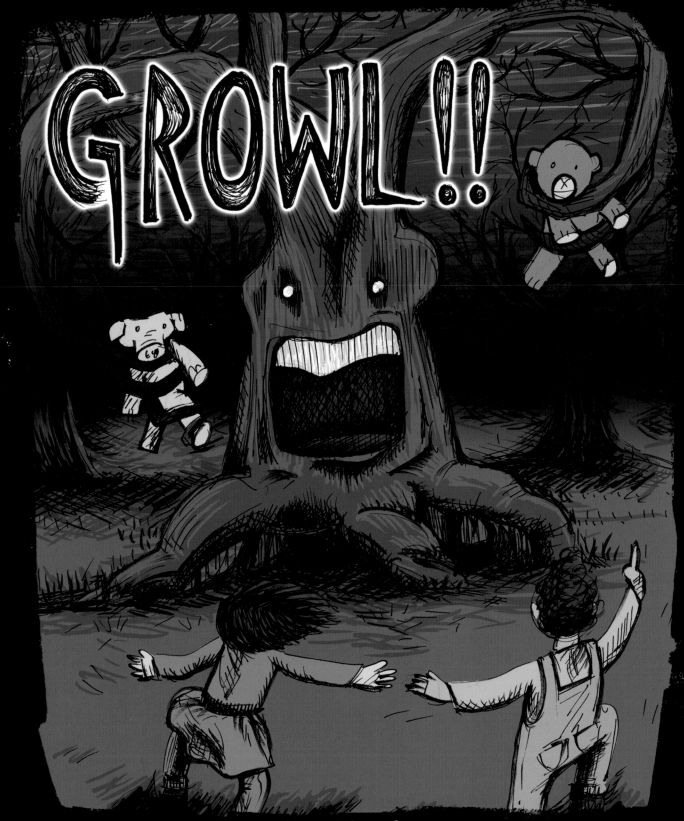

I looked at Piggy and Teddy's faces.

"WE NEED TO BE BRAVE."

I got on my tippy toes and raised my arms high.

He didn't get scared!

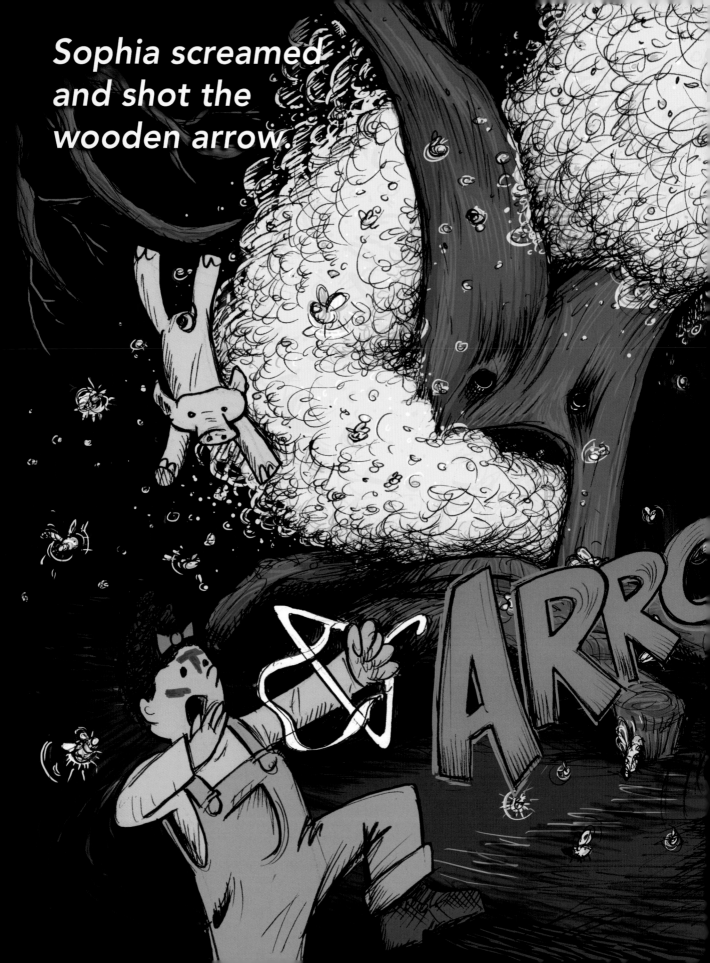

The creature dropped Piggy and Teddy, then **BURST** into fireflies and **DASHED** into the night sky.

Piggy gave me a big hug. "I will always keep you safe," I told him.
Teddy gave Sophia a huge smile. "I will always protect you,"
Sophia promised.

We skipped back to our cabin, and as we passed the boys' cabin, I sang, **"See, WE are FAMOUS monster slayers!"**

After we climbed into bed, I kissed Piggy

and Sophia kissed Teddy.

And together, we fell fast asleep.